ISBN 978-0-06-304055-7

The artist used an iPad Pro and the app Procreate to create the digital illustrations for this book.
Typography by Erica De Chavez
21 22 23 24 25 PC 10 9 8 7 6 5 4 3 2 1
❖
First Edition

Dedicated, with love,
to our little monsters Finn,
Dashiel, Eleanor, and Delilah. And
for all the "meanies" out there, we
see you, we love you, well done!
—K.H. & J.S.

For Joanne and Pam
—P.B.

Hey, all you **DUDES AND DUDETTES!!**
Let me set up the **DRAMA**.
I am the kid,
and *that* lady's my **MAMA!**

Some moms are **LOUD?!**
Some live for caffeine.
Some moms enjoy hiking—
But my mom . . . is **MEAN!**

Mommy wakes me up with tickles and turns on the LIGHT.

Then I slump into the kitchen,
where she's singing a song.
She makes me my breakfast,
but she does it all wrong!

Breakfast one is too
BRIGHT.

Breakfast two is too
SCARY.

Breakfast three is *nearly* right,
but the eggs look sorta
HAIRY.

"Get dressed! It's school pictures!"
—an unpleasant surprise—
"Remember, no scowling,
no frowning, no crossing your eyes."

She puts balm in my hair.
It just makes me look greasy.
My shirt is too itchy.
And the creases? Too creasy!!

We head to the gymnatorium after math, robotics, and art.
The microphone is ready for the spelling bee to start.

Oh no. It's my mom in the very front row.
And she's holding a sign that says

After all that hoopla, I only come in eighth place.
But Mom is there cheering like it was an Olympic track race!

At lunchtime, I sit down
with grumbles in my tummy.
I open up my lunch box
to all kinds of cool yummies.

After school, it's not over.
In fact, it's more confusing.
Mom says one thing, does another—
I don't find it amusing.

"Be careful, little one,
water can be a DANGER."
But then she makes me take swimming
twice a week with a STRANGER!

At home, she's a nutball.
"Leave your shoes at the DOOR!"

I bolt to my chair.
This meal IS MY JAM!
Milk, blueberry muffins,
and beef stew—
"More? Yes, Ma'am!"

I know it's a bribe,
so "we can chat" while we eat.
She asks a GAZILLION questions,
like an interrogation
in HEAT.*

*Yes, the 1995

crime drama

HEAT.

"BATH, BOOKS, AND BED,"
she says, with hands on her hips.
She says it like five hundred times,
until she has veeerrry thin lips.

Once out of the bath, it's time for night-nights.
I keep telling that woman, "They're getting *tight-tight!*"

"You're growing too fast!"
And then her lips start to shake.

"If you want me to SLOW MY GROW,"
I say, "then let me eat cake!"

We get into bed, my favorite half hour.
I select eighty-two books, piling them high as a tower!

Mom is so mean
that we only read four!
But I'm so awed by
her character voices
that she gives me
an encore.

On my back, she draws wiggles and squiggles.
She calls me SHMOOPY POO.

Okay, *that* isn't so mean.
It is just something that we do.

She kisses my forehead
and puts her cheek next to mine.
As I roll into Sleepytown,
my heart-lights start to shine.

Someday, I will have a kid of my own.

And mark my words,
WHEN I DO, I am going to be
the MEANEST
MOM OF ALL...
Because being mean . . .
means . . .